Planet Puzzle

Lee Aucoin, *Creative Director*
Jamey Acosta, *Senior Editor*
Heidi Fiedler, *Editor*
Produced and designed by
Denise Ryan & Associates
Illustration © Kimberly Scott
Rachelle Cracchiolo, *Publisher*

Teacher Created Materials

5301 Oceanus Drive
Huntington Beach, CA 92649-1030
http://www.tcmpub.com
Paperback: ISBN: 978-1-4333-5562-2
Library Binding: ISBN: 978-1-4807-1707-7
© 2014 Teacher Created Materials

Written by Bill Condon
Illustrated by Kimberley Scott

It's perfect weather for a picnic on Saturn!
Robo-Pilot knows all the shortcuts. If we miss space
jams and falling stars, we'll be there in a wink and
a blink!

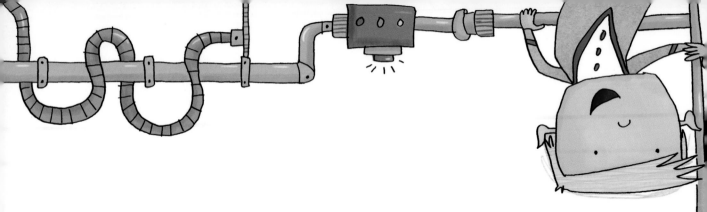

Papa grins. "You won't be bored today, kids, because we're going to play Planet Puzzle!" A huge round planet appears on a screen. It's called Earth.

"Twenty points for each correct answer and the first to a hundred wins a trip to a moon with a ride on the Lunar Leap!" Mama says.

"First question—what is all that blue you see on Earth?" asks Mama.

Amarissa quickly says, "Blue paint!"

"No, absolutely wrong!"

"Blue cheese?"

"No, Amarissa," says Mama.

"Can you give us a clue?" asks Zachariah.

"Okay. It starts with *W*."

"Blue whales?"

"No."

"Blue wwww. . .woodpeckers?"

"Nice try, Zachariah. But no."

Zachariah and Amarissa are my brother and sister. I'm a year older, which means I'm also a year smarter. "My turn," I say. "This needs brains."

"So how are you going to answer it?" asks Amarissa. The twins giggle, but I'll show them!

I twist my head around so I can look at the planet upside down. It looks exactly the same. Hmm, I try to think of something starting with *W*. I've got it! "Worms! Earthworms! Blue ones!"

"No, Saskia," says Mama. The twins giggle. Again!

11

Papa spins his ears to get our attention—that always works. "The correct answer," he says, "is water!"

Mama tells us that more than seventy percent of Earth is covered in water. That's liquid water—it's not in tablet form like ours. It's found above ground, and Earthlings drink it!

Only one word describes how I feel about all this— INCREDULOUS!

"Are Earthlings real, Mama?" asks Amarissa. "I thought they were just in made-up stories."

"Very real. There are billions of them."

"Cool! I wish we could see what they look like."

"You can," Mama smiles. "Let's zoom in on Planet Earth."

15

Suddenly, Earth is close up. There are Earthlings everywhere! Zachariah points at the screen. "They aren't wearing anti-fume shields!"

"Earth's air isn't like ours," Papa explains. "Earthlings can breathe it as often as they like. And they don't turn green or burst into flames."

"There's something I don't understand." Amarissa frowns. "Earth is a sphere, right Mama?"

"Yes."

"Well, why don't Earthlings fall off their planet?"

"That's easy," says Zachariah. "They put glue on their shoes, like we do."

"No, that's wrong," Mama replies.

At last I have a chance to show how clever I am! "I know. I read about it once," I say.

"Tell us, Saskia," says Mama.

"Earth has gravy!" I say proudly.

"Well, the answer is actually *gravity*," Mama says. Zachariah and Amarissa laugh.

"I was close!" I protest.

"Oh dear," Mama sighs. "You're not doing very well, children. I think we should stop playing Planet Puzzle."

"No!" wails Amarissa. "We have to play until we get a hundred points."

"So we can win a ride on the Lunar Leap," adds Zachariah.

Papa shakes his head. "Sorry, that might take a long, long time."

Mama turns off the screen. "Thanks for playing, kids."

"Saturn is sooo far away." I yawn. "Are we there yet?"

Mama squeezes my hand. "No, Saskia, we're not even out of the spaceport yet."

I groan. The twins do, too.

But then, with a whirr and a whoosh, we're off! We shoot out of the spaceport, over the Milky Way Bridge, and straight past Space Junk Mountain!

"What's going on?" I ask. "This isn't the way to Saturn. We're heading to the moon."

"Change of plans." Mama winks at Papa. "We thought we'd give you a little surprise."

"That's right," says Papa. "You're all going for a ride on the Lunar Leap!"